be

LO...

LOVE

FROM

'TOPS'

12/'02

The
Weather Fairies™

Illustrated by

Margaret W. Tarrant

Original poetry by

Marion St. John Webb

Series Editor
Fiona Waters

·MARGARET TARRANT'S· TM

FAIRIES & FLOWERS

First published in this format in 2002 by
The Medici Society Ltd
Grafton House, Hyde Estate Road, London NW9 6JZ

Copyright © The Medici Society Ltd 2002 / 1927

First published in 1927 by The Medici Society Ltd
1 3 5 7 9 10 8 6 4 2

The rights of Margaret Tarrant and Marion St John Webb to be identified
as the Illustrator and Author of this work have been asserted by them in
accordance with the Copyright, Design and Patents Act 1988

A catalogue record for this book is available from the British Library

ISBN 0 85503 256 1

Margaret Tarrant's original artworks have been rescanned for this re-designed edition.

Designed by Tony Potter Publishing Ltd

Printed in Singapore

The
Weather Fairies™

Margaret Winifred Tarrant (1888 - 1959)

'Every time a child says, " I don't believe in fairies," ' warned Peter Pan, 'there is a little fairy somewhere that falls down dead.' Through her paintings Margaret Tarrant did as much to stop this happening as J M Barrie in his writings. Born in London in 1888, the only child of artist Percy Tarrant, Margaret was 19 when she illustrated Charles Kingsley's *The Water Babies*. Her delicate pictures earned her important commissions: *Nursery Rhymes*, *Alice in Wonderland* and *Hans Andersen's Fairy Tales*.

Between 1915 and 1929 she illustrated some 20 books for George G Harrap & Co., and for The Medici Society produced some of her best-known work, including - in the 1920s - this famous series of fairy books. Her picture of *Peter's Friends*, inspired by J M Barrie's *Peter Pan* stories, proved extremely popular, and in 1921 her *Do You Believe in Fairies?* caught the public excitement created by Sir Arthur Conan Doyle's *The Coming of the Fairies.*

During her life Margaret Tarrant tackled a wide range of subjects, but her forte was fairies, in which she could express her love of children, wild flowers and dance. She would sketch meticulously from life, then arrange the subjects in imaginary settings, infusing them with a distinctive otherworldly quality.

Margaret Tarrant was very much a free spirit herself, flying along the country lanes around her home in Surrey on her bicycle, leaping off to sketch a flower. She never married, but attracted many friends by her zest for life. Perhaps it was this childlike enthusiasm, combined with a special imagination, that gave her an affinity with fairies. When she died in 1959, she left a lasting legacy in charming pictures that still enchant new generations with their glimpses into a secret fairy world.

Contents

What will the Weather be? ... 9

The Sunshine Fairy's Song ... 15

Caught in the Curtain ... 21

A Postcard from a Fairy ... 27

At the End of the Rainbow ... 31

The Tale of Jack Frost ... 37

Fairies in Art ... 44

Other books in the series ... 46

What will the Weather be?

North Wind,
South Wind,
East Wind,
West Wind,
Blowing all together!
What will be the weather?

Said the North Wind Fairy:
"Today the cold North Wind shall blow,
And bring the frost and hail and snow.
And all the early flowers shall quiver,
And little girls and boys shall shiver!
    The cold North Wind shall blow!"

Said the South Wind Fairy:
   "No, no. The South Wind blows today.
   So soft and warm and sweet I say.
   And clouds shall part and dewdrops
      shimmer,
   And children laugh and sunbeams
      glimmer.
      The South Wind blows today!"

Said the East Wind Fairy:
   "Give me a chance! Give me a chance!
   I'll make the children skip and dance.
   I'll pinch their toes and make them hurry.
   And set the world a-scurry-flurry.
      Come, come, give me a chance!"

Said the West Wind Fairy:
   "Today the wet West Wind shall blow,
   And bringing rain, shall make things
      grow;
   And roads shall fill with mud and puddle,
   While men in mackintoshes huddle.
      The wet West Wind shall blow!"

So each wind insisted he must blow, blow,
      blow.
"Which way?" cried the Weathercock.
      "Which way do I go?
   North Wind?
      South Wind?
         East Wind?
            West Wind?
   Blowing all together!
   What *will* be the weather?"

The
Sunshine Fairy's Song

The Sunshine Fairy's singing
  As she flies across the land.
And all the little flowers
Look up and understand.
She sings to them,
And brings to them
A message full of cheer.
"Greetings to you all," she says,
"The Sunshine Fairy's here!"

In every hole and corner
Where the Shadow Fairies hide,
She stops, and slips in quickly -
And drives them back outside.
She flies to them,
And with a gleeful shout
Cries out loud "Never mind!
Come out and face the world
   with me,
And leave your cares behind!"

The Sunshine Fairy's singing
As she gently glides along.
And every dream in all the world
Is safe inside her song.

Caught in the Curtain

Two bad and naughty fairies,
    While playing one bright day,
Caught a tiny little elf -
And hid him quite away,
Rolled him in a curtain of mist -
And said it was just play.

But then the curtain rolled up.
And inside it was squeezed
The poor tiny little elf.
The fairies were so pleased.
"You'll have to stay there now
For ever," they teased.

Well - at first the elf laughed,
And rolled all about.
And he thought it a game,
And good fun, no doubt.
But then at last he got tired,
And he wanted to get out.

He pulled at the curtain.
He gave it a twist.
He tried with his feet, and
He tried with his fist.
But he *couldn't* get through
The curtain of mist.

He tried to be brave, but
His heart was filled with fear.
He struggled and he shouted,
But no one came near.
Then down from his eye there rolled
One huge, great, big, tear.

It splashed through the curtain
And it made a large hole.
And through this strange doorway
The elf he quickly stole,
And ran back to his mother,
The poor little soul!

The bad and naughty fairies
Said one to the other,
 "Just think, my dear!
Sometimes, it would appear,
A smile is less useful
Than one huge big tear!"

A Postcard from a Fairy

Snowflakes, sprinkling, falling,
Can you hear the fairies calling,
The fairies in the woods, among the trees?
They watch you tumbling, dropping.
And call you, without stopping,
To ask, "Have you a message for us, please?"

Snowflakes twirling, swirling,
You are fairy postcards, whirling
From the fairies in the clouds to those below.
Soft you float, each light and airy,
Down to a waiting fairy,
Who grasps and reads her postcard made
  of snow.

It's true - for Jack Frost says it's so.
But what he will not tell us though -
And what we really want to know -
Is how the woodland fairy sends
A postcard to her cloudland friends?

At the End of the Rainbow

If you want to be a fairy
    You should simply look around,
For when you reach a rainbow's end -
You will see, waiting to be found,
A pair of gleaming fairy wings,
Sparkling on the ground.

So put them on, then count up to ten -
Smile, and you're a fairy then!

Some people shake their heads.
"No, not wings," we're told.
"Lying at the rainbow's end
You'll find a pot of gold!"
The people who believe in this
Are not like us, they're too old.

But we believe in fairy things,
And we shall find those sparkling wings.

The
Tale of Jack Frost

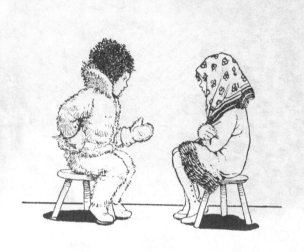

This tale of Jack Frost is so chilly
and cold,
You'd best put on your gloves while it's told,
And shut tight the window, and while the
flame's red,
Sit close to the fire with a scarf round
your head.

Now, if you're quite ready
We'll start on the tale . . .

It starts at midnight, with wind,
  snow and hail,
When down the street Jack Frost
  came creeping,
While all the good folk in the village
  were sleeping.
He took from his pocket a brush, and he said,
"I'm going to paint pictures, all out of
  my head.
But not of that which around me I see,
I'll picture the world as I'd like it to be!"

He started to work, and he painted away
On the villagers' windows, till break of day.
And the pictures he drew were a
    wonderful sight -
All sparkling and gleaming, and crisp
    and white.

"Now that should cheer people up," he said
As everyone lay sleeping and dreaming
in bed.

At the last cottage he paused, then took up
    his brush
And drew one more picture, in a bit of a
rush,
On a window that looked over a high
    brick wall,
And that picture he drew was the best one
    of all.
And then, as the sun rose, he hid by a tree.
"I must hear what is said when my work
    they see."

The man in the cottage, he got out of bed.
He yawned, rubbed his eyes, looked round
    and said,
"Oh look, Jack Frost has been here in
    the night,
And drawn on my window, what a
    wonderful sight!"

And he smiled at the picture, the best one
   of all,
For Jack Frost had hidden the high
   brick wall.

Jack Frost gave a laugh, his thin face alight,
And, smiling, he turned and crept away
   in delight.

Fairies in Art

The dusk of the nineteenth and dawn of the twentieth centuries were magical times for fairy lovers. Fascination with fairy lore was widespread, reaching unprecedented heights in 1922 when Sir Arthur Conan Doyle published *The Coming of the Fairies*, containing 'photographs' of fairies taken by two young girls in a Yorkshire village.

This interest was mirrored in an outpouring of art and literature. Children's books cultivated belief in fairies: they were used in religious teaching, magazines were devoted to them, and captivating new works appeared, most notably J M Barrie's *Peter Pan* and *Peter Pan in Kensington Gardens*. Rudyard Kipling wrote *Rewards and Fairies* and even Beatrix Potter embraced the subject in *The Fairy Caravan*.

Artists revelled in the opportunity to portray imaginary worlds. Arthur Rackham, the most fashionable illustrator of his day, depicted a sinister fantasy landscape, peopled by spiky goblins, fairies and mice amid gnarled trees with gnomelike faces. In contrast, Honor Appleton, Maud Tindal Atkinson and Mabel Lucie Atwell offered gentler, comforting images recalling Kate Greenaway's illustrations of apple-cheeked children.

The two names most associated with fairies in the 1920s and 1930s were those of the friends and sketching partners, Margaret Tarrant (1888-1959) and Cicely Mary Barker (1895-1973). Both began to use Art Nouveau and Arts and Crafts elements in their work, and in Tarrant's paintings a breathtaking attention to detail – diaphanous wings with the intricate tracery of a dragonfly's wings - is a testament to the reality of fairies, imaginary or otherwise.

Other books in the series

FLOWER FAIRIES
First published 1923

FOREST FAIRIES
First published 1925

SEED FAIRIES
First published 1923

WILD FRUIT FAIRIES
First published 1925

SEASHORE FAIRIES
First published 1925

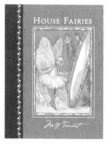

HOUSE FAIRIES
First published 1925

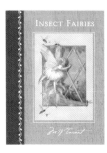

INSECT FAIRIES
First published 1925

WATER FAIRIES
First published 1925

HEATH FAIRIES
First published 1927

WEATHER FAIRIES
First published 1927

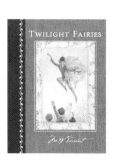

TWILIGHT FAIRIES
First published 1928

ORCHARD FAIRIES
First published 1928

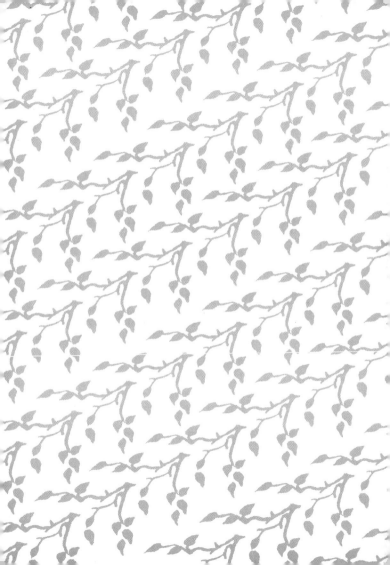